Copyright © 1988 Jean Ure
Illustrations © 1988 Michael Lewis
First published 1988 by Blackie & Son Ltd

British Library Cataloguing in Publication Data

Ure, Jean, 1942 –
Two men in a boat.
I. Title II. Lewis, Michael III. Series
823'.914[J]

ISBN 0-216-92336-0

Blackie and Son Ltd
7 Leicester Place
London WC2H 7BP

Printed in Spain
SALINGRAF, S.A.L.

TOWN AND COUNTRY STORIES

Two Men in a Boat

JEAN URE AND MICHAEL LEWIS

Blackie

Ben and Simon were digging a hole to
Australia. They had been digging all day
and still they had not got there.

'I know!' cried Ben.

He had had an idea. In the corner of the garden stood a big spade. It was just the sort of spade for digging holes to Australia!

Ben fetched the big spade and started to dig. Suddenly, as he dug, the hole began to fill with water.

The water welled up, higher and higher,
until it had welled right over the top. Next
it began trickling its way down the garden.

'This is GOOD!' shouted Ben. 'Now we
can SAIL to Australia!'

If you were going to sail to Australia, then you needed a boat. There must be a boat somewhere in the garden! Ben ran off to look for one.

In the garden shed he found a log and a ball
of string. They would do!

Ben ran out of the shed. 'Look what I've
got!' he cried. Simon looked. He saw a log

with a piece of string tied round it. Ben
pulled the log across the grass and set it
down with a plop in the water.

'This is the good ship Benjamin,' said Ben.

Of course! Simon could see it quite clearly
now. A fine big sailing ship to take them to
Australia!

'Are you ready, Mr Mate?' said Ben.

Simon looked round to see who he was
talking to.

'You!' said Ben. 'I'm the Captain, and you are my Mate. And when I say, *are you ready*, you must say, *ay, ay, sir*!'

'Ay, ay, sir!' said Simon.

'Then all aboard!' cried the Captain. 'Full steam ahead!'

They sailed down to the bottom of the garden and over the wall to the river beyond.

The river was deep, and dark, and full of gloom. Thick branches grew overhead, and strange, slimy, creepy creatures wriggled and lurked in the depths below.

'Ahoy!' cried the Captain. 'Crocodile ahead!' The Mate gulped, and clutched at the Captain's hand. As they sailed past, the crocodile opened an eye. The Mate waited, trembling, for the snap of jaws. What would it feel like to be eaten alive by a crocodile?

Fortunately, the crocodile didn't seem to be
hungry. 'I expect it's just had its dinner,'
said the Captain.

The Mate nodded, carelessly. It was not
that he had been scared — but he was glad,
all the same, that the crocodile had not
wanted to eat him!

From the bank came the sound of rustling.
WHAT WAS THAT?
A wild, spitting creature burst through the bushes. It stood there, glaring at them.
'Sabre-toothed tiger,' said the Captain.
The Mate felt his knees begin to wobble.
'I'll tell it to go away,' said the Captain. 'Shoo!' he told the tiger.

The tiger opened its mouth and snarled.
For a terrible moment the Mate thought it
was going to spring, but then, with an
angry swish of the tail, it turned and
bounded off.

The Mate gave a little swagger. He had
not been scared!

'Yo ho!' cried the Captain. 'There's the sea!'
The Captain raised his telescope to his eye.
'And over there,' he said, 'is Australia.
Would you care to take a look, Mr Mate?'

The Mate held the telescope to his right
eye and did his best to close his left eye as
he looked through it. Whenever he closed
his left eye, his right eye closed too. Never
mind! He could see just as well without the
telescope.

On the sea shore were some natives. There was a brown furry native lying on its back with its paws in the air, and two girl natives. The girl natives were standing on their heads, with their skirts falling round their ears so that you could see all their knickers. Red knickers and blue knickers. How rude!

'Ahoy there!' shouted the Captain. 'Is this Australia?'

The girl natives looked at each other.

'Yes,' they said. 'This is Australia — and this is our kangaroo!'

The kangaroo sat up and scratched itself. Then it lay down again, and rolled on its head.

The Mate plucked at the Captain's sleeve.
'Why are they all upside-down?'

'We're not upside-down,' said the native
in the red knickers. 'You are!'

'Yes,' said the other native, 'what are you
standing on your heads for?'

The natives giggled.

'Where have you come from, anyway?'
said Red Knickers.

'We've come from England,' said the Captain.

'Oh, well, that accounts for it! Everybody in England stands on their heads. It's because of being underneath.'

England wasn't underneath! It was Australia that was underneath.

'If you want to come ashore,' said Blue Knickers, 'you'll have to learn to stand the right way up.'

'I'm afraid we don't have time just now,'
said the Captain. 'We have to get back
home, you know, to have our tea.'

Oh, the Mate was relieved!

'Up anchors,' cried the Captain. 'Splice
the mainbrace, Mr Mate!'

'Ay, ay, sir!' cried the Mate.

Back across the sea they sailed, and back up the deep and gloomy river. Then splish-splosh, up the garden path.

'Bread-and-jam-and-cocoa,' they chanted as they sploshed. 'Bread-and-jam-and-cocoa-and-a-nice-hot-bath!'

But a nice hot bath is the one thing they cannot have. There isn't any water! All the water has run away, down the garden path.

Someone has been digging and has burst
the water pipe.

   Now the only water left is a little tiny
drop from the bottom of the kettle . . . Ugh!
What a horrid cold way to have a nice hot
bath!

'Next time you go to Australia,' said their mother, as she tucked them into bed with their bread-and-jam-and-cocoa, 'you'd better go by jumbo jet!'

Wherever did she think they were going to get an elephant from?